BEASTIE BROS

Published in the UK by Scholastic, 2026
Scholastic, Bosworth Avenue, Warwick, CV34 6UQ
Scholastic Ireland, 89E Lagan Road, Dublin Industrial Estate, Glasnevin, Dublin, D11 HP5F

ISBN 978 0702 34448 0

A CIP catalogue record for this book is available from the British Library.

Printed in the UK.
Paper made from wood grown in sustainable forests and other controlled sources.

FSC www.fsc.org MIX Paper | Supporting responsible forestry FSC® C018072

10 9 8 7 6 5 4 3 2 1

www.scholastic.co.uk
For safety or quality concerns:
UK: www.scholastic.co.uk/productinformation
EU: www.scholastic.ie/productinformation

David O'Connell

BEASTIE BROS

The CURSE of CAPTAIN SLUGBEARD

SCHOLASTIC

For Jamie & Lil

BUGTOWN

TO THE CABBAGE FOREST
THE BEEHIVE
TO THE DUNG HEAP
DASH'S TREE HOUSE
THE MUSEUM OF COOL STUFF
DRIBBLE'S WORKSHOP
BUGTOWN SQUARE
THE TINKLE
GROTTIBOTTIGAN'S
POLICE STATION
TO SLUGSVILLE
THE ANT HILL
TO BEETLEBOROUGH

BEASTIE BROS CAST

REG SCRIBBLE

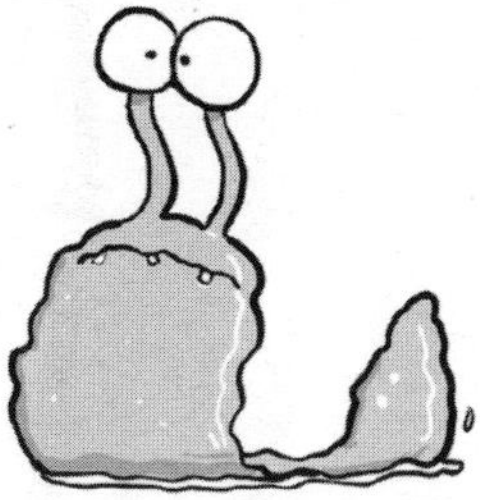

FLATTENED DOMINIC

LOU

NETTY

MR TRUFFLE

PRUDENCE

CAPTAIN SLUGBEARD

SGT BUZABIZ

Toot
TWANG
COLA
PONG
CHUNKS
YOU'RE ENTERING
Bugtown

CHAPTER ONE

BUGTOWN! It's the place where every bug is your friend. Except the biting, stinging ones that want to eat you, lay their eggs inside you or give you a disease, of course! Those ones aren't your friends, although they might be your neighbours, or even your relatives...

If you want to meet a less creepy sort of creepy-crawly, the best place to visit in **Bugtown** is **Grottibottigan's Juice Bar** – home of the

Bin-Juice Spritz. All the best bugs go there! You can have a delicious nettle and mushroom smoothie, chomp on some snacks – cabbage crispies, bark chips or perhaps a slime toastie? – and maybe even take part in a spot of karaoke.

Grottibottigan's is where Dash the firefly found himself one morning, along with his best frenemy, Gus the housefly. They were having a competition to see who the most annoying talker could be, or at least that's what it felt like to Dash. Gus was winning comfortably, droning on about his new air fryer.

"I've become quite the chef," he said. "The **Lard-Blaster XL** has two compartments, so I can make salty scabs and deep-fried dandruff flakes at the same time." Gus would eat anything.

Dash yawned over his custard and cauliflower smoothie (custard was his favourite thing). "That's so interesting," he said, though he didn't really mean it.

Dash loved food – in fact, if he went too long without eating, he turned into a terrifying, mindless creature known as a hunger-zombie. But listening to Gus talk about his air fryer was in danger of driving him mindless too.

Luckily, Dribble the snail squelched into the juice bar at that moment.

"Hello, bro!" Dribble said, grinning.

Dash breathed a sigh of relief, and his bottom lit up, which it always did when he was happy. Dribble wasn't just Dash's best friend, he was also his adopted brother. The two had grown up together and got into all sorts of adventures. Even though Dribble could be a bit grumpy sometimes, he was a lot more fun than Gus.

The snail tried to order his usual cabbage juice from Cool Nat, the bartender, but Nat was very busy and not his usual cool self at all.

"I'll be with you in a moment, dude!" he said, running from a blender to the bar with a pineapple chunk and back again. "My helper,

Janice the moth, is in hospital after an avocado-related injury, so I'm managing the juice bar by myself."

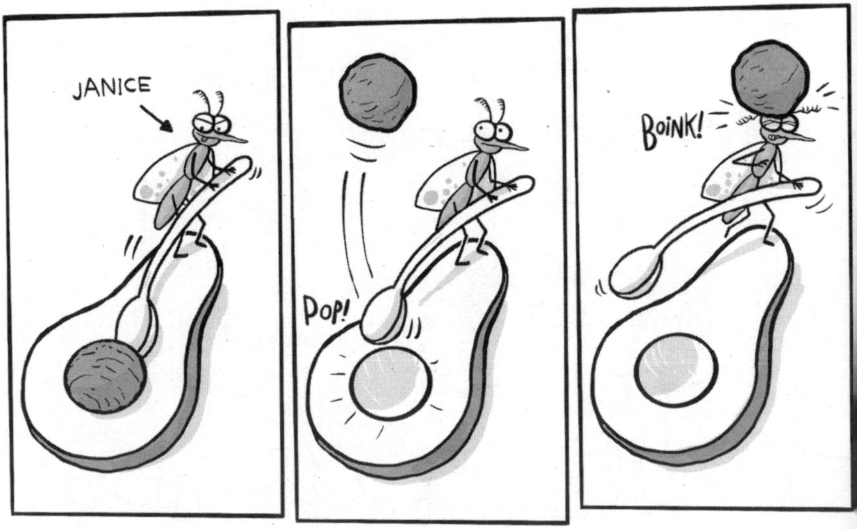

"Oh dear!" said Dash. "Poor Janice."

"That's not all," said Frazzled Nat. "I need to practise for the **Juice Barista Championships** next week. I'll be mixing my signature smoothie in the **Coolest Smoothie** competition – I call it the 'Surf and Turf' – and it needs to be perfect-o!"

"You're sure to win!" said Dash. "How could anybody not love your smoothies?"

"Even if you have to wait ages for them," muttered Dribble.

He perched himself on a stool next to Dash and Gus while he waited for his drink. He had a look on his face that Dash knew well. It was a look that involved shining eyes and a smug smile, which is quite difficult to pull off when you're a snail and your eyes are on stalks and your mouth is next to your belly button. It was Dribble's "I've just invented something" look.

Dribble was always inventing things in his workshop, but his inventions only seemed to work in a way that left a giant, smoking crater in the ground and scorch marks on nearby buildings and people. Dribble's inventions made Dash nervous.

"It's very quiet in here..." Dribble said. This was not true as Grottibottigan's was actually *full* of bugs, all waiting for drinks. Not only that, but Taneesha the stick insect was also on the karaoke stage singing her version of "Butterfly Blues", and she had a voice like a chainsaw slicing a piano in half.

"What this place needs is some *fizz*," Dribble finished.

He did his smug smile again. He was hinting at something. That was when Dash saw the object stuck to Dribble's belly.

Dribble didn't have hands, as he was a snail, but he used his snail slime to hold things if he needed.

"What's that?" asked Dash.

"Oh, this?" said Dribble innocently. "It's my latest invention."

Gus took a long swig of his Bin-Juice Spritz. "How long have we got until it explodes?" he said.

"I'm sure it's brilliant, whatever it does," Dash said supportively, although he was secretly thinking the same thing as Gus.

Dribble plonked the gadget on to the bar dramatically. "This is the **Bubbler**," he announced.

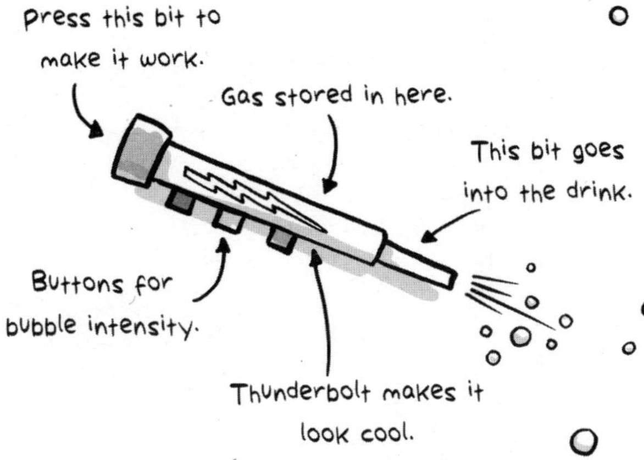

"You stick one end of it into your drink, press a button, and it fills the drink with bubbles and makes it fizzy! Smoothies, juices, tea, gravy, pond water – whatever you like! I thought Cool Nat might like to try it out."

"That is an unusually sane idea of yours, dude," said Cool Nat, bringing Dribble his glass of cabbage juice.

Nat eyed the **Bubbler** like it might bite him, but carefully picked it up and poked it into the cabbage juice. He pressed the button and, with the noise of someone blowing their nose, the gadget shot out a blast of bubbles that made the juice froth and foam – and spill over the sides of the glass.

"It might need some fine-tuning," admitted Dribble. "But it does work."

Cool Nat then used the **Bubbler** on Dash's and Gus's drinks.

"I like the fizziness," said Dash, taking a sip. "But it makes my smoothie taste funny."

"That will be the fart gas I use to create the bubbles," said Dribble. "Midge farts are the bubbliest type."

Dash decided he didn't want any more smoothie, but Gus gulped his drink down.

"Very tasty," he said with an extra-bubbly burp.

Cool Nat was also unsure. "Fart-flavoured drinks are not everyone's cup of tea, dude," he said. "And the **Coolest Smoothie** award is my priority for now."

Dribble looked downhearted. No one ever took his inventions seriously.

Dash was as wary of destruction and the taste of farts as anyone, but he felt sorry for his brother. What could he do?

Just then, Taneesha came up to the bar.

"Singing makes you thirsty," she said. "I'd like a seaweed juice, please, Nat."

"Coming up, dude," said Cool Nat. He went to fill his blender with ingredients, but the colour suddenly drained from his green face.

"I'm all out of seaweed!" he cried. "It's an ingredient in my Surf and Turf smoothie and I've used it up already. I need it for my practice mixes, but I don't get my seaweed delivery until next **Wormsday** – which is after the competition!"

"But it's my favourite," said Taneesha. "And **Wormsday** is days away."

SURF AND TURF SMOOTHIE RECIPE

Ingredients:
seaweed, grass, compost, seagull poo

Add all ingredients to a blender. Blend on high speed until a thick green slimy pulp is produced. Serve over ice. Enjoy!

"It's a disaster! The seaweed comes all the way from **Bogbrush-on-Sea**. I'd get it myself, but with Janice in hospital, I'd have to shut the juice bar while I was away. And where would **Bugtown** be if Grottibottigan's was closed?"

Everyone gasped. It was unthinkable.

Dash suddenly had an idea.

"If we go and get your seaweed from **Bogbrush-on-Sea**," he said, "would you give Dribble's **Bubbler** a trial run at Grottibottigan's?"

Nat grinned. "It's a deal! If you bring me the seaweed, I'll trial the **Bubbler** and give you free drinks for a month!"

Dribble's face lit up.

"Thank you, Dash," he said. "What a brilliant plan! I've never been to **Bogbrush-on-Sea**. It'll be like a little holiday."

"Did he say free drinks?" said Gus. "In that case, I'll help too. I'll make some snacks in my air fryer to take with us."

"And I'll make a playlist of songs," said Taneesha, "so we can have a singalong on the way."

"Wonderful," said Dash, who was having second thoughts already.

"It'll be a proper road trip!" cried Dribble. Then his face fell. "There's only one thing wrong with the idea."

"What's that?" said Dash.

"We don't have a car. So how are we going to get to **Bogbrush-on-Sea**?"

WANTED
WANTED

CHAPTER TWO

As the four friends left Grottibottigan's, Dribble was filled with gloom.

"If we don't get that seaweed, there's no chance Nat will use my **Bubbler**," he said as they walked, flew and slithered down the street.

"And Nat needs to practise for the **Juice Barista Championships**," Dash pointed out. "He works so hard at Grottibottigan's he deserves to get an award!"

"But we'll need a big car to get the four of us and a load of smelly plants back to **Bugtown**," said Gus. "In fact, we'll need a van or a truck or a bus! Where are we going to find one of those?"

"Hmmm!" said Dash. He'd had another idea. "Reg Scribble and Flattened Dominic have a bus. Maybe we could borrow it."

"Those rascally slugs will never let us use their bus," grumbled Dribble. "Not unless they get something out of it in return. Slugs are like that."

Reg and Flattened Dominic ran a tour bus business – when they weren't breaking the law by thieving or helping other criminals. Dribble and Dash didn't approve of the slugs, even though Reg's girlfriend was Tilda the nice earthworm. Tilda insisted the slugs were turning over a new leaf, but so far the new leaf hid a troublesome bush full of old leaves.

"We've no other options," said Taneesha, "so it's worth a try. Let's go and ask them."

They soon found the spot where the slugs' bus was normally parked. The bus was empty of passengers. A bored-looking Reg was leaning against its door.

"Ahoy, landlubbers," he said when he saw the four friends. Reg had spent time at sea and called everyone "matey" or "landlubber". He was covered in tattoos of mer-slugs and sea monsters. "You're just in time for a tour of the sights of **Bugtown**."

"We live in **Bugtown**," said Gus. "We already know the sights."

"We'd like to go somewhere else for a change," said Dash.

"Somewhere else?" said Reg, as if the idea of a tour bus leaving **Bugtown** was the strangest thing he'd ever heard. "Where do you have in mind?"

"How about **Bogbrush-on-Sea**?" said Dribble. "Just for a quick seaside trip to get some ... souvenirs." He thought it best not to mention the piles of smelly seaweed that would be coming back with them.

Reg's eyes shone. "**Bogbrush-on-Sea**!" he said. "I've had many a mischief-making misadventure

there, matey. Seaside trips could be a smart next move for the business. I can see it now: **Slugtours Sunshine Holidays**. We could turn the bus into a camper van! Climb aboard, landlubbers, and let's be off!"

They piled into the bus, waking Flattened Dominic, who was draped over the steering wheel, fast asleep. He'd once been run over by an escaped courgette so was often mistaken for a puddle or a net curtain.

"Set course for **Bogbrush-on-Sea**, D-Flat, matey!" commanded Reg as the others took their seats. "With a quick stop on the way to pick up the love of my life."

"Your pickle collection?" said Dominic, confused.

"No – the fair Tilda!" said Reg. "The second ... I mean, first love of my life."

*

Tilda was very surprised to see all her friends on board the bus when it stopped outside her house a short while later.

"What a lovely day out!" she said when they explained the plan. She quickly threw some food, cups and plates into a picnic bag, and the tour bus set off again.

The sun was shining as they drove out of **Bugtown** and into the countryside. Everyone was in a good mood.

"This has been easy, so far," whispered Dribble to Dash as the bus chugged on its way. "If the rest of the trip goes as smoothly, we'll be back in **Bugtown** in no time, and my **Bubbler** will soon be fizzing up all the drinks in Grottibottigan's. Finally, one of my inventions will be taken seriously!"

The good mood didn't last long, however. The travellers soon noticed the traffic around them getting busier and busier, and eventually the bus came to a standstill.

"What's going on?" asked Dribble. "We'll never get to **Bogbrush-on-Sea** at this rate!"

At that moment, they heard a motorbike weaving its way through the cars behind them.

Dash leant out of a window and saw it was their friend Sergeant Buzabiz on his police bike.

"Hello there," said Sergeant Buzabiz, stopping next to the bus. "It looks like you're in a bit of a jam. That reminds me..." He got off the bike, took a jam doughnut out of his pocket and started munching on it.

"Why isn't the traffic moving?" asked Dash.

"I heard on the radio there's a pigeon having a nap on the junction ahead," the police bee said casually. "It's blocking all the important roads. Everyone's tooting their horns, but it won't wake up, so you'll just have to wait."

"But we need to get to **Bogbrush-on-Sea**," said Dribble. "It's urgent! It's a matter of life and death. Well, not life and death, but seaweed and ... bubbles!"

Sergeant Buzabiz chuckled. "You young bugs are always in a hurry," he said. "As it happens, I'm heading to **Bogbrush-on-Sea** myself. There's a police conference taking place at the **Bedbug Hotel** for the next few days." He finished his doughnut and hopped back on to his motorbike. "I'll see if I can help shift the pigeon. Have fun at the seaside!"

The police bee carried on his way, nipping in and out of the tiny gaps between the stationary cars.

"It's all right for some!" muttered Dribble. "He'll be in **Bogbrush-on-Sea** long before us."

"We could have a singalong to pass the time," suggested Taneesha.

"No, thanks!" said everyone else quickly.

"It's almost lunchtime," said Tilda. "Why don't we have the picnic I packed?"

"It doesn't seem right to have a picnic in a bus," said Gus, who wasn't normally fussy about where he ate. He was usually quite happy in a toilet bowl. "We should be outside."

"Let's have it on the roof," said Flattened Dominic. "There's plenty of room up there."

He opened the bus door, and the passengers

clambered on to the roof. Tilda and Reg set out the picnic, while Dribble rummaged around in his shell until he found a beach umbrella. The snail's shell was mysteriously a lot bigger on the inside, and Dribble said he'd found the umbrella in the "second attic". Everyone helped themselves to food, and Dribble even used the

Bubbler to put some fizz in the drinks. The bugs were soon enjoying themselves. The weather stayed fine, and they had a nice view over the countryside and of all the annoyed drivers glaring up at them enviously.

"I can see the pigeon far ahead," said Taneesha, who was the tallest. "It's still fast asleep.

Is it time for that singalong yet?"

"No!" said everyone at once.

"Then let me tell you all a tale from my time at sea," said Reg, a rascally twinkle in his eye. "This talk of **Bogbrush-on-Sea** has got me remembering my adventures as a sailor, when the one thing I feared – apart from hungry seagulls and generally getting wet – was being hunted by villainous cut-throat pirates!"

Tilda gasped in horror. "Pirates!" she said. "I didn't think they still existed!"

"Oh yes, my sweet landlubber," said Reg. "And none are more villainous or more cut-throaty than the dreaded Captain Slugbeard..."

"Captain Slugbeard?" said Dash. "I thought he was just a story."

"He's more than a story, matey," said Reg. "He's alive and as slippery and dangerous as an electric eel! Slugbeard and his crew of the good ship **Norovirus** spread terror across the seas, stealing and plundering as the mood takes them. The **Norovirus** often sneaks into **Bogbrush-on-Sea**'s harbour. The rumour is that Slugbeard has a hideout on an island somewhere nearby, but no one's ever found it."

"Have you ever met him?" asked Taneesha.

"Yes indeed, landlubber. The captain is covered in scars from all his battles, and he has a gold tooth and a beard longer than my nan's. It's a fearsome face I hope never to see again!"

"Why?" asked Dash.

"Because I pinched his wooden leg."

There was a stunned silence.

"He didn't need it, to be fair, as slugs get by perfectly well without legs," said Reg. "But I don't think he was happy, all the same."

"I don't believe a word of it!" muttered Dribble. "It's a load of bumguffery! Except maybe the bit about stealing." He gave Reg a disapproving look.

"We'll never find out whether he's real or not," said Gus. "Not if we don't get out of this traffic jam."

There was still no sign of movement from the sleeping pigeon.

"Would anyone like some jelly?" asked Tilda. "I've a bowl in the picnic bag. It's pond-scum flavour, freshly made today."

"Oh, yes, please!" said Dash, who loved jelly almost as much as he loved custard. He took the bowl from Tilda's bag, but as he stepped backwards, he stood on Dribble's tail by accident.

"OW!"

the snail cried with a jolt, and he accidentally dropped the **Bubbler** into the bowl. The gadget burst into life with a snort, making a cluster of bubbles in the jelly. The bowl lifted off the bus roof, and Dash had to grab it quickly before it flew away.

"We almost lost the jelly!" he said.

"And my invention with it!" Dribble complained, flexing his sore tail. "The midge fart gas is lighter than air. The bubbles will keep going up and up until they pop!"

"Hmmmm," said Dash, rubbing his chin thoughtfully. "I wonder..."

He suddenly clambered down from the

bus's roof, taking the bowl and the **Bubbler** with him.

"What are you up to?" Dribble said.

"Wait there," Dash called up. "I think I might know a way out of this traffic jam!"

The puzzled bugs peered over the side of the bus, trying to see what Dash was doing. The little firefly stood inside the vehicle and pressed the **Bubbler** into the jelly. Green bubbles erupted from the bowl like transparent jelly beans, floating upwards until they were trapped by the ceiling. Very soon, the bus was filled with jelly bubbles, glistening in the sunlight through the windows.

"I can feel the bus moving," said Dribble.

"It's taking off!" cried Taneesha.

Dash sneaked out of the bus, quickly

closing the door behind him to trap the bubbles, and flew back up to the roof.

Sure enough, the bus was slowly rising into the sky, lifted by the gas-filled bubbles. It floated gently over the surrounding cars, their astonished passengers watching open-mouthed as the flying bus left them behind.

"What a brilliant idea!" said Dribble. "It's almost at my level of genius!"

"Let's set sail for **Bogbrush-on-Sea**!" cried Reg happily. "Except we don't have sails."

"How exactly do we drive this thing?" asked Dominic.

"Gus and I can use our wings to steer," said Dash. "All we have to do is follow the road to **Bogbrush-on-Sea**."

The two little flies hung on to the back of the bus, buzzing their wings whenever the bus needed to change direction. They swiftly passed

DROPPIT & SMASH
REMOVALS

over the sleeping pigeon and went onwards, towards the sea.

"Wheee!" said Tilda as they flew over a hill. "This is amazing!"

But Dribble wasn't very happy. "No, it's not," he said, squeezing himself inside his shell. "Snails are meant to be on the ground! Let me know when it's all over."

It wasn't until late afternoon that they saw the sparkling sea ahead, with the little bug village of **Bogbrush-on-Sea** nestled beside it.

"Drop the anchor, shipmates!" cried Reg, who was really getting into the spirit of things.

"He means, how do we stop?" said Flattened Dominic, looking below the bus nervously.

Dash knew what to do, though. He flew

back down inside the bus and began to pop the jelly bubbles, one at a time. As each bubble burst, the bus sank a bit closer to the ground. Gus kept the bus steadily on course.

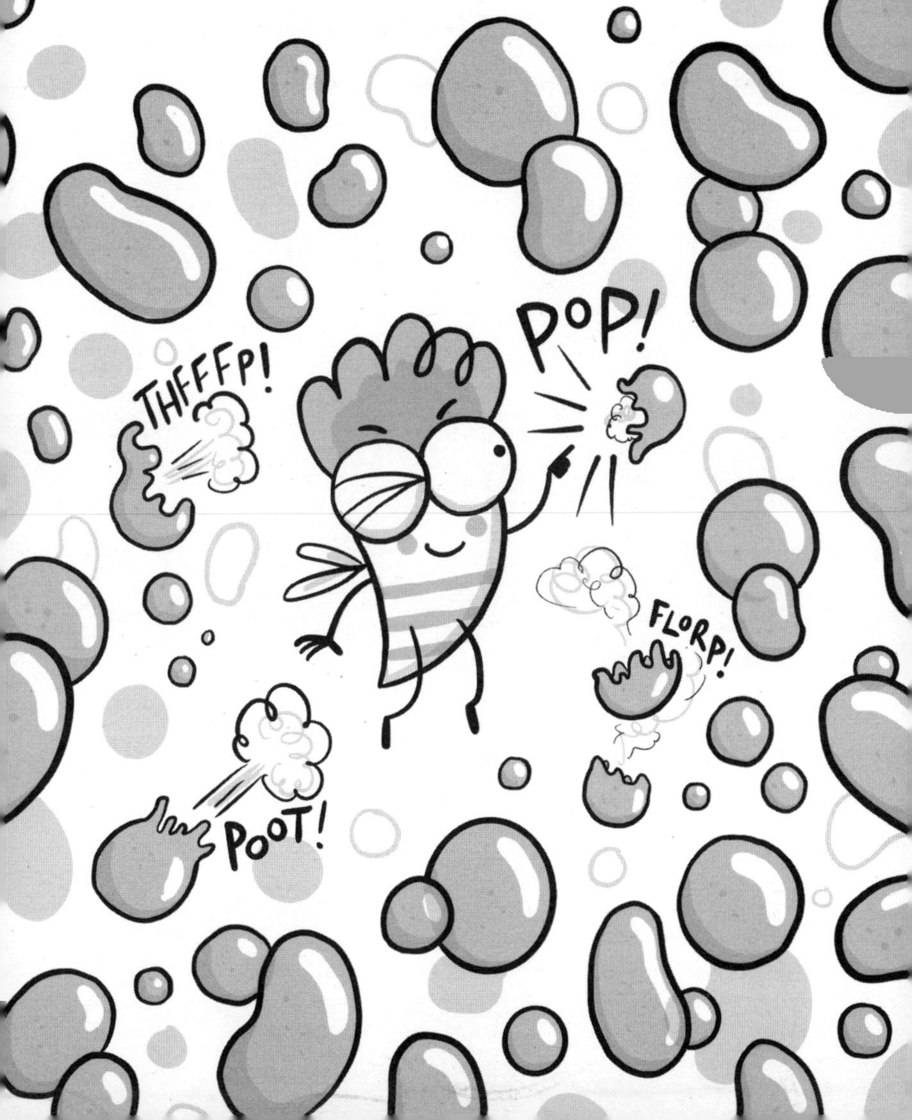

"There's a parking spot near the **Bedbug Hotel**!" said Dominic. "We can land there."

As Dash popped the final bubble, the bus landed on the ground with a bump. Dribble, still in his shell, rolled from the roof and fell into Dash's waiting hands. A shaky eye poked out of the shell.

"Let's never do that again!" he said.

The bugs took in the view. **Bugbrush-on-Sea** looked like a great place to stay. As well as the hotel, there were some cafes and shops overlooking a long stretch of sand. At one end of the beach was a pier with amusements and, at the other end, a lighthouse. There were also lots of holidaymakers who were packing up after a day at the seaside.

"It will be getting dark before long," said Dribble. "We'd better be quick about collecting the seaweed so we can take it back to Grottibottigan's."

"By the time we get back to **Bugtown**, the juice bar will be shut for the day," Taneesha pointed out. "And I don't fancy looking after a load of seaweed overnight, even if it is used to make my favourite drink."

"We can get the seaweed tomorrow morning and then go back to **Bugtown**," said Dash. "Nat will still have time to practise for the competition. Anyway, I think the bus will need to be aired overnight to get rid of the midge fart smell!"

At that moment, the slugs reappeared, having gone to investigate the hotel.

"The hotel manager is a matey of mine from my seafaring days," said Reg. "He's managed to find us some rooms at a cheaper price."

"Although the place is full of police,"

added Dominic, "so we'll have to be on our best behaviour!"

"Does the hotel have a spa?" asked Gus, who loved a sauna with fluffy towels.

"A spa, a restaurant and even a maggot crèche," said Reg. "It'll be like a proper holiday."

The bugs trooped into the hotel. It wasn't very grand, but they were glad to have somewhere to stay. There were lots of police bugs buzzing around, busy with their conference.

But this made it all the more surprising when Dash spotted three guests that he recognized. They were the very last people he'd expected to see...

CHAPTER FOUR

Dash gave Dribble a nudge.

"Look!" he hissed. "It's them. And they're not even in disguise!"

"It can't be!" said Dribble.

But it was. Sitting in the lounge, without a care in the world, were a couple of familiar dung beetles and a large dung ball. They were Netty, Lou and Mr Truffle, otherwise known as the Dung Heap Gang, a bunch of criminals that Dribble and

Dash had run into a couple of times before. The beetles and their dung-ball mastermind were reckless thieves who liked nothing more than drama and attention, and they'd certainly picked the right place for it this time!

The beetles saw the brothers and waved. They didn't seem very bothered that they were surrounded by police.

"I can't believe you're here!" said Dash, marching over. "Don't you know there's a police conference going on in this hotel?"

"That's why Mr Truffle chose it," said Netty, giving the dung ball an adoring smile. "We're lying low and needed somewhere to hide out. The police would never think of looking for us here."

"It's the perfect place," continued Lou with a chuckle. "Right under their noses!"

Bugs don't have noses – but if they did, having Mr Truffle right under them would not have been particularly pleasant. The dung ball just sat quietly, blending in with the other tourists.

"We ought to tell the police about you right now!" said Dash, fuming.

The beetles pouted.

"Please don't," said Lou. "We haven't done anything naughty in ages. We're thinking of leaving our criminal careers behind."

"Going to prison would be very awkward," said Netty. "Won't you give us a chance?"

Dribble and Dash looked at each other.

"I don't know why I'm standing up for them," said Dribble, "but the slugs have made a new life for themselves. Maybe this lot can too."

"All right," said Dash with a sigh. "But if we hear of any trouble, we'll turn you in!"

The beetles nodded meekly.

Just then, there was a rumble of thunder outside.

"There's a storm brewing, shipmates!" said Reg gleefully. "It will be a perfect night for telling

stories around the fireplace – stories of pirates and treasure."

"Or for watching TV in our rooms," said Gus, trudging to the lift.

"Or a singalong?" said Taneesha.

"No, thanks!" said everyone.

*

After some dinner in the hotel restaurant, Dribble and Dash went up to their room, but over the course of the evening, the storm grew. The brothers could hear the wind howling and the waves crashing on the beach. The rain poured down, the thunder roared and the lightning flashed.

"I don't like storms!" said Dribble, quaking under the bed covers. "Sitting around the fire telling stories seems like a good idea after all. It has to be better than listening to this inconsiderate weather."

The two went down to the hotel lounge and found Taneesha, Gus, Tilda and the slugs gathered around the fireplace. Sergeant Buzabiz and his police friends were nearby, eating doughnuts and telling jokes, mostly about pigeons blocking roads. The Dung Heap Gang were also sitting at a table, playing cards. Mr Truffle appeared to be winning, which was annoying the beetles.

"Reg was telling us more about Captain Slugbeard," said Tilda as the brothers joined them on the sofa. "It's very exciting!"

Reg grinned, enjoying the attention. "My matey the hotel manager was saying there's not been a sighting of Slugbeard in a long time," he said. "But the captain always comes back after a storm to check on his treasure. He buried his pirate booty on the beach, you see. The storm might wash the sand away, allowing others to find it."

11:58

"It's a bit daft, leaving your riches on a beach," said Gus. "Why doesn't he have a bank account like everyone else?"

"Because he's a pirate!" snapped Reg. "Pirates don't have bank accounts. It's not a very pirate-y thing to do. And you can't put a curse on a bank account."

"A curse?" said Dash. Reg's stories were always a bit colourful, but this one was painting a rainbow.

"A curse of bad luck!" said Reg darkly. "Anyone who steals the treasure from its hiding place will suffer a terrible misfortune."

"What kind of misfortune?" asked Flattened Dominic, who considered himself quite experienced when it came to the subject of bad luck.

"Well, I don't know," muttered Reg, who didn't like getting bogged down with details. "Meeting a very angry pirate, probably. Being made to walk the plank. That kind of thing."

"What a load of nonsense!" said Dribble. "There's no such thing as curses."

Suddenly thunder shook the building and lightning flashed in a particularly spooky, crackly way.

Dribble squeaked in fear. "Don't hurt me, Captain Slugbeard!" he cried. "I promise not to touch your treasure!"

"Don't worry, Dribble!" said Dash. "You said it yourself. There's no such thing as curses. And there's nothing magical about Captain Slugbeard. Even if he is real, he's just a slug with a boat and a bad attitude."

"Anyway, we won't meet him," said Taneesha cheerily. "Tomorrow we'll be back in **Bugtown**, all safe and sound."

The storm began to quieten and soon everyone went off to bed for the night.

Everyone except the Dung Heap Gang, who had been listening to the conversation with interest...

That night, Dribble had a horrible nightmare about gold-toothed pirates chasing him across a stormy sea, and a treasure chest that opened like a mouth and wanted to eat him. He also dreamed about a dancing pineapple called Sandy, but that might have been the cabbage-flavoured cheese he'd had for dinner.

By the next morning, the storm had died out. After breakfast, Dribble and Dash went straight to the beach to look for seaweed. The slugs were having a business meeting together in the lounge, while Tilda and Taneesha were visiting the shops, and Gus was having his bum waxed in the hotel spa. But they all said they would definitely help out as soon as they were free.

"The storm will have washed lots of seaweed up on to the shore," said Dash, "so it shouldn't be hard to find. Once we've collected it, we can return to **Bugtown**."

"And not a moment too soon," grumbled Dribble. "I'm already fed up with **Bogbrush-on-Sea**. It's been nothing but storms, pirates and curses since we arrived. And dancing pineapples. I thought the seaside was supposed to be fun."

"At least the sun's out now," said Dash, trying to cheer his brother up. "And look at all this!"

Dash was right about the seaweed. It was scattered everywhere, covering the sand. The sea had also washed up plenty of other things too, like shells and pieces of broken wood. There were rock pools all around them, full of brightly coloured stones and strange plants.

The brothers were so busy looking at everything they didn't notice that they were being followed...

The two bugs had soon gathered plenty of seaweed. Dribble was much happier when he saw the large pile of salty plants they'd made, even though it did smell a bit.

"This should keep Cool Nat busy making smoothies for the rest of the year!" he said. "He'll win his competition, then he'll trial my **Bubbler** and realize how brilliant it is, and then he'll ask for a load more **Bubblers** to be made. And then my genius will be appreciated by everyone!"

"Yes, probably," said Dash, dumping some more seaweed on the pile. Then he stopped. "Did you hear that?" he asked.

"What?" said Dribble. "Not more thunder? My nerves can't take any more storms."

"No," said Dash. "Listen."

They both stood still. There was a faint cry coming from further down the beach, near the shoreline.

"Help!"

"Someone's in trouble!" said Dash.

"I can't see anybody," said Dribble, stretching his eyes as far as he could.

"Help!"

Dash took off, flying towards the voice. There was a rock pool not far away, cut off from the sea by a stretch of sand. A forlorn-looking creature peered out from the water. She had a whiskery face and a pair of claws.

"There's someone stuck in the rock pool!" he called to Dribble.

The snail hurried over to the edge of the pool.

"It's some kind of sea bug," said Dribble as Dash landed on a rock nearby.

"I'm not a bug," said the creature, swimming about irritably. "I'm a prawn. My name's Prudence and I've been trapped here all night. Rock pools are nice for a visit, but now I want to get back out to sea."

"What happened?" asked Dash.

"I was battered about all over the place in the storm," Prudence explained. "A huge wave swept me in here. It seemed like a safe place to stay, but after the storm calmed down I discovered I had no way of getting out again. I'm not made for walking on land, and I need to get back to my home in **Shrimpville**."

"We'll help," said Dash immediately. "We just need to figure out how. I'm not sure we can carry you. We could do with another big wave to take you back to sea."

"We could be waiting here all day," said Prudence. "Or at least until the next storm!"

"No more storms!" cried Dribble. "All that howling wind."

"Wind!" said Dash excitedly. "We need a gust of your wind, Dribble!"

"I've plenty," the snail grumbled. "That cabbage-flavoured cheese I ate for dinner was deadly."

"I mean, wind from the **Bubbler**!" Dash said, his bottom lighting up in excitement. "If you stick the **Bubbler** in the rock pool and turn it up to full power, the gas could blow up a wave that lifts Prudence out of the pool and back into the sea."

"What did you say?" said Prudence, her eyes popping out of her head. "Gas?"

"It's just bottled fart gas," said Dash reassuringly. "I'm sure it's only slightly explosive. Nothing to worry about at all."

"It's bonkers, but it's worth a try," said Dribble.

He took the **Bubbler** out of his shell and poked it into the pool.

"Brace yourself, Prudence!" he warned the prawn.

He set the **Bubbler** to maximum power and pressed the button.

FFFFLLAAARRRRPPP!

It was the loudest fart **Bogbrush-on-Sea** had ever heard. Its epic power created a giant fountain of water that blasted Prudence out of the pool in an instant, and sent her shooting back into the sea

with a splosh. Huge clouds of sand, dust and seawater were kicked up into the air and rained down upon the beach.

Dash stared at the **Bubbler** in surprise.

"I think it worked," said Dribble, shaking sand off his shell.

"I'm freeeeee!" cried Prudence, leaping in and out of the surf. "Thank you so much, land bugs! I will never forget your help – though it's going to be a while before I wash off that fart smell." With a wave of her claw, the prawn swam away and soon disappeared.

"At least we've done a good deed today," said Dash, his bum beaming with happiness.

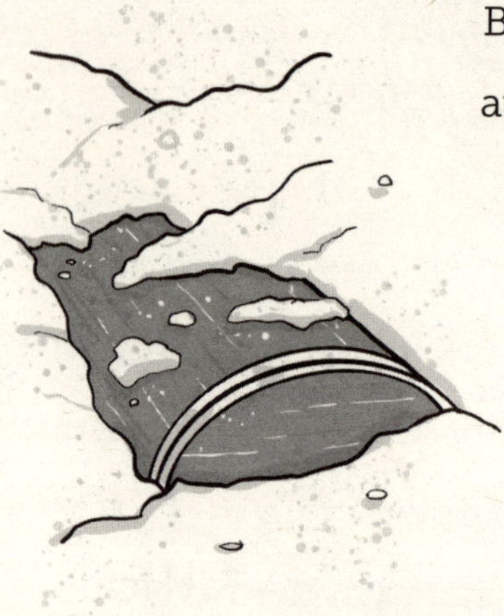

But Dribble wasn't paying attention. He was staring at something sticking out of the sand nearby.

"What's that?" he said. "It looks like a box of some kind."

"Hmm. It must have been buried out of sight, and the **Bubbler** has blown the sand clear," said Dash. "I wonder what it is!"

Dribble disappeared inside his shell and emerged a few moments later with a spade.

"I found this in the tool shed," he said.

Dash grabbed the spade and began digging around the object. Before long, he had uncovered a large wooden chest.

Dribble gasped in horror.

"It's a treasure chest!" he cried. "Oh no! It must be the hoard of Captain Slugbeard. The pirate treasure that Reg was telling us about!"

"Perhaps it's just a box," suggested Dash. "What does that writing on the lid say?"

"I be the property of Captain Slugbeard," Dribble read.

"I'll admit that doesn't sound good," said

Dash. "But it's hardly conclusive. It could be a laundry basket. Anything else?"

"Lay a finger on this treasure chest and ye shall suffer a terrible fate. Dash – what shall we do?"

"Maybe there's another Captain Slugbeard," said Dash, still clutching at a rather feeble straw. "Maybe he has a brother who's *not* a fearsome pirate."

"Don't be silly!" said Dribble, his voice full of panic. "We've found Slugbeard's treasure and now we're cursed! Woe is me! I'm too young to die!"

"Curses are nonsense," said Dash calmly. "It was just a tale made up by the pirates to scare people away. We could bury it again. No one would know."

"But we know," said a voice behind them.

Dribble and Dash turned to see three figures appear from behind some rocks. It was Netty, Lou and Mr Truffle – the Dung Heap Gang!

"We knew you'd go looking for the treasure," said Netty, edging closer. "Mr Truffle said we

should follow you, and he was right!"

"We weren't looking for the treasure!" said Dash. "We found it by accident. We were collecting seaweed."

"Whoever heard of such a thing?" said Lou, rolling her eyes. "But you've saved us the bother of digging up the treasure ourselves. We'll take that, thank you very much!"

Before Dribble or Dash could do anything, Netty and Lou grabbed the chest and hauled it over to Mr Truffle, who glared threateningly at the brothers.

"I thought you were leaving your criminal careers behind!" said Dash angrily, shaking

his fist. "We're going straight to the police."

"We'll be long gone by then," said Netty with a wicked smile. "And, anyway, this treasure is already stolen, so it doesn't count. Finders keepers!"

"But what about the curse?" said Dribble.

"How many times, Dribble?" said Dash. "Curses aren't real."

"You could always ask them if it's real," said Lou.

"Ask who?" said Dash.

"Those pirates," said Lou, pointing out to sea. "The ones sailing right towards us...

NOROVIRUS

CHAPTER SIX

Dribble and Dash turned to see a huge wooden sailing ship slicing through the waves and making straight for the beach. A black flag with a skull and crossbones flew from the top of the mast – which was odd because bugs don't have skulls or bones.

"It's Slugbeard and his cut-throat pirate crew!" screeched Dribble. "This is the bad luck we were warned about!"

"But Reg said the curse took effect if you pinched the treasure," said Dash. "And we haven't done that. The beetles have."

The two turned back to look at the Dung Heap Gang, but Netty, Lou and Mr Truffle had vanished, along with the treasure chest.

"We'd better get out of here as well!" said Dribble.

But it was too late to escape unseen. A small boat had set out from the ship, rowed by a crew of tough-looking bugs, and it was already reaching the shore. Standing at its prow was a large, scowling, bearded slug. Scars covered his face, and he wore a black feathered hat on his head and had a cutlass in his sword belt.

"You there, you maggoty deck swabs!" cried the slug, slithering towards them.

"I think he means you," whispered Dribble, nudging Dash.

"I means both of you, you slippery salmon-spit," snarled the slug, flashing his gold tooth. He eyed the brothers suspiciously. "I'm Captain Slugbeard, the terror of the tides. Why are you earth-plodders loitering around here?"

"We've been collecting seaweed," said Dash truthfully. "Our friend needs it for his juice bar."

At that moment, the pirate spotted the hole in the sand where the chest had been buried and his eyes bulged.

"A likely story!" growled the slug. "What have you ludicrous, lolloping landlubbers done with my treasure? I left it right here! Tell old Slugbeard, or I'll turn you into juice and feed your gizzards to the gizzard-eating thingy of the deep."

The pirate crew behind him laughed nastily.

"We found your treasure by accident, Mr Slugbeard," squeaked Dribble, trembling. "And then it was stolen by a criminal mastermind and his accomplices. You've just missed them!"

"Another likely story," said the slug. "And it's Captain Slugbeard to you, pipsqueak!"

"Please don't curse us, Captain Slugbeard!" whimpered Dribble. "We'll splice your mainbrace or shiver your timbers, or whatever else you want! Just let us keep our gizzards. I don't know what they are, but I don't want them fed to anything!"

"What I want is my treasure!" cried Slugbeard. "I knew I should have opened a bank account instead of leaving it buried on the beach. You two feeble excuses for fish fingers are my prisoners until you tell me what you've done with it. Take them away!"

"But we haven't—" Dash began, but the pirates wouldn't listen.

With a "yo-ho-ho", the pirate crew grabbed Dribble and Dash, and carried them off to the

rowing boat, which then launched out to sea, towards the waiting ship. The brothers huddled together as the pirates pulled on the oars, steering the boat over the waves. What fate lay before them?

The crew said nothing, but eyed their prisoners menacingly and spat on the floor at their feet – which was very unhygienic, but the pirates were obviously too tough to use tissues.

The ship's masts towered over them like angry trees as the rowing boat approached. Dash could see the name **Norovirus** painted on the ship's side, and a figurehead of a mermaid with stomach cramps decorating the prow. It was a proper pirate ship, just like the ones in movies!

The pirates dragged them on board and tied them to one of the masts.

"Where are you taking us, you villains?" said Dash bravely.

"We're setting sail for our pirate lair on **Crabsick Island**!" said Captain Slugbeard. "Then I'll decide what punishment you'll suffer. You can be sure it'll be slow and painful but also entertaining."

The pirate bugs all gave loud toothless laughs before readying the ship for the voyage.

"What can we do?" said Dribble miserably. Even though he was pretty slimy, he couldn't wriggle free of the rope. "I don't want to be slowly, painfully but entertainingly punished!"

"Don't worry, Dribble," said Dash firmly, though he was starting to get pretty worried himself. "We'll think of something."

The crew hauled up the anchor and the ship set off, passing **Bogbrush-on-Sea** on its way. The pirates began loudly singing a sea shanty, just to be extra annoying.

"Look, there's Reg, Flattened Dominic and the others!" said Dash excitedly as the ship skirted close to the harbour. "Maybe they can get help!"

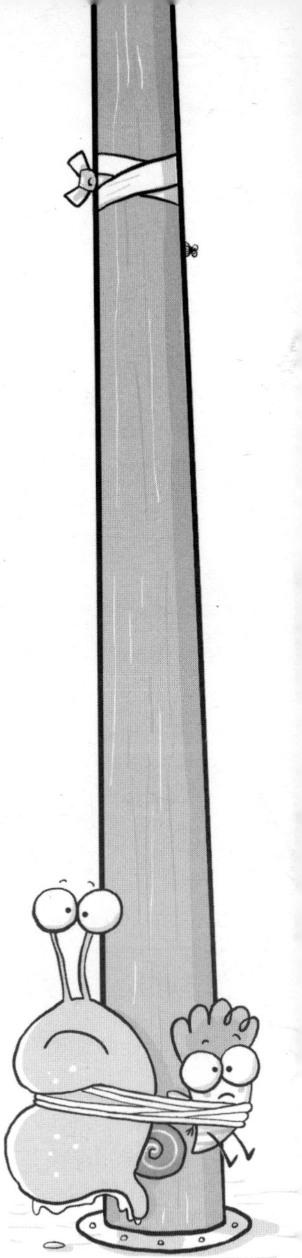

Dribble and Dash desperately shouted to their friends, who were on the harbour wall, admiring the view.

"Help!" cried Dribble. "We're being bug-napped by pirates!"

Tilda saw them and waved her tail.

"Are you going for a cruise around the bay?" she called. "Don't be too long, because we have to get back to **Bugtown** this afternoon."

"It's not a cruise ship!" yelled Dribble. "They're pirates!"

"I can't believe you're having a singalong without me!" called Taneesha.

"They're pirates!" Dribble repeated. "And we're tied up! Help!"

"It's a bit rude to go on a musical cruise without us," shouted Gus grumpily. "Are there snacks?"

"**NO!**" yelled Dribble. "**WE'RE BEING BUG-NAPPED BY A BUNCH OF TUNELESS CUT-THROAT PIRATES, YOU DAFT, BUZZING, WINDOW-BOTHERING GERM JOCKEY!**"

"It's useless," sighed Dash. "They can't hear us over the noise."

"You'll get no help from them, you slimy soil crawlers," cackled Slugbeard. "And especially not from that two-faced jellyfish bogey, Reg Scribble. I've still not forgiven him for stealing my wooden leg. **Crabsick Island**, here we come!"

Dribble and Dash could only watch helplessly as the **Norovirus** sailed further away from the safety of land and headed out to open water.

"We're up to our necks in trouble now," said Dribble. "If we ever get out of this mess, I'll never leave Bugtown again."

"I hate to bother you with more bad news," said Dash, "but I'm starting to get a bit hungry."

Dribble gulped. This was bad news. Whenever Dash became hungry, he transformed from a friendly firefly into a hunger-zombie.

When he was in that state, he would eat anything – including snails. Dribble desperately tugged at the ropes. If he didn't untie himself soon, he could end up as a snack!

Just then, there was a shout from a lookout high up in the crow's nest.

"Ahoy, Captain!" they called. "There's a fin poking up above the water not far off the starboard side!"

The colour drained from Slugbeard's face.

"A fin!" he gasped. "Do you mean...?"

"Aye, sir. It's Big Steve – and he's heading this way!"

"Big Steve?" said Dash.

"Be afraid, landlubber," said Slugbeard, grinding his teeth. "Be very afraid. Big Steve is the biggest mullet you've ever seen, and I don't mean the dodgy haircut! He's a fishy horror who haunts these waters like a silver phantom. Many ships have been lost to his mighty jaws and dagger-like teeth. And he has a taste for pirates, as my crew have discovered."

Dribble and Dash glanced at each other nervously. If the pirates were afraid of this creature, then it must be truly terrifying!

Suddenly they saw a huge fin cutting through the waves towards the **Norovirus**. The crew ran about the deck in alarm, attempting to steer the ship out of its way, but then the fin disappeared under the water and there was a **THUMP** as the ship was hit by something underneath it. The deck shook and the mast wobbled, and the crew cried out in fear.

"He's trying to knock the ship over!" Slugbeard said. "He'll be back for another go!"

"What shall we do, Captain?" said one of the terrified sailors. "Big Steve won't stop until he's made a meal of us!"

Slugbeard slowly turned to look at Dribble and Dash. "Then maybe we'll give him what he wants," he said.

CHAPTER SEVEN

"Untie the prisoners!" Slugbeard commanded.

"Actually, there's no need," said Dribble desperately. "We're quite happy where we are. In fact, this mast is rather comfortable."

The crew ignored him and freed both Dribble and the now very hungry Dash.

At that moment, there came a shout from the lookout:

"Big Steve is coming back, Captain!"

The giant fish swam at the ship, getting

faster and faster. He raised his head out of the water, showing off rows of sharp teeth.

"Say your farewells to each other before we chuck you overboard!" said Slugbeard.

"Now would be the perfect time for a good idea, Dash!" squeaked Dribble as he was dragged to the side of the ship.

But Dash didn't answer. He twitched and began to drool. His eyes became wild, and his teeth were growing into fangs...

"FOOD!" was all he said.

DISASTER – he'd turned into a hunger-zombie! He wasn't good for anything now! Dribble was on his own.

The pirates were too busy to notice and simply pulled zombie-Dash across the deck to join his brother.

"Make them walk the plank!" cried Slugbeard. "That's what you get for stealing my treasure!"

The pirate crew scurried around on his orders, placing a length of wood over the side of the ship. Dribble and Dash were shoved along the plank towards its edge.

Big Steve was getting closer by the second.

"FOOD!" growled Dash, eying his brother.

"Not now, Dash!" said Dribble. "I don't know which is worse: being eaten by a fish or being eaten by your own brother! Especially when I'd rather not be eaten at all."

Without warning, Big Steve burst out of the water. In a flash of silver scales, he knocked the startled bugs right off the plank. Dribble screamed as he fell straight into the monster's open mouth, which shut with a snap.

"FOOD!" gurgled Dash as he tumbled into the water. In his zombie state, he had no fear, only hunger. He grabbed Big Steve's tail. "YUMMY FISH!"

He sank his fangs into the huge tail and took a bite out of it. Big Steve would have cried out in pain if he hadn't had his mouth full of snail. Instead, the monster's eyes bulged, and he spat

AAIEEE!

Dribble straight back out again with such force that the snail shot up on to the deck of the ship, landing with a squelch.

"Yuck!" said Dribble, trembling in horror as fish saliva dripped off him. "I'll never eat sushi again!"

Meanwhile, Big Steve was trying to shake Dash off his tail, but the little hunger-zombie wasn't letting go. The fish furiously thrashed around in the water, Dash clinging on with his fangs the whole time. Big Steve began to panic – perhaps he'd met his match with this tiny bug! He swam in circles round the ship so that it tossed about violently.

Finally, with a powerful flick of his tail, the fish threw Dash high into the air so that he too somersaulted back on to the **Norovirus**. Who needed wings with that kind of service? The startled crew caught Dash as he landed, still chomping happily on a leathery piece of fish tail.

With a bitter snarl, Big Steve disappeared beneath the waves. He'd had quite enough of these annoying bugs for now. But he was still hungry...

"I feel much better after that," said Dash, who had returned to normal now that he'd eaten. "And I've had a nice refreshing swim too."

Slugbeard was staring at the little firefly in amazement. "I've never seen anyone take on Big Steve like that!" he cried. "There's more to you vermin than meets the eye, that's for sure."

"Dash saved the ship and its crew. And me as well, more importantly," said Dribble. "Are you going to free us in return?"

"No!" snapped the captain. "There's still the matter of my missing treasure."

At that moment, Slugbeard spotted the **Bubbler**. Dribble had been quaking so much from his ordeal that it had fallen out from inside his shell and landed on the deck beside him.

"Are you hiding some booty from us, you dollop of fish-flob?" growled Slugbeard, eyeing the metal gadget. One of the pirates scuttled forward to scoop up the **Bubbler** and showed it to the captain.

"Hands off my booty!" cried Dribble. "I mean, hands off my **Bubbler**. It could be my most important invention yet!"

"If it's valuable to you, it's valuable to us!" said Slugbeard, tucking the **Bubbler** underneath his hat. "We'll add it to our loot, to make up for the missing treasure. You two are coming with

us to **Crabsick Island**, whether you like it or not. I'll decide what to do with you there."

With the wind behind it, the ship sped on its way. Soon they saw an island looming ahead of them. But as they drew nearer, the brothers noticed it was actually a gigantic raft floating on the sea, made up of bits of wood and broken ships lashed together.

"That explains why no one has ever found Slugbeard's hideout," whispered Dash. "**Crabsick Island** isn't an island. It's a boat that can move wherever the pirates want it to!"

"They're cunning rascals!" said Dribble. "We're going to have to think of a really genius plan to get out of this one, Dash. And how to get my **Bubbler** back too!"

The **Norovirus** moored at a wooden jetty, and the prisoners were led along its salt-worn boards and into a rickety building that had a sign with "**Captain Slugbeard's Secret Hideout**" written on it, just in case anyone was unsure. The building creaked like a lobster with a stiff leg as it gently bobbed upon the sea.

"Take them to the cells," Captain Slugbeard said.

A burly beetle pirate tugged open a trapdoor and pushed Dribble and Dash through it into a

cage that hung from a rusty chain. The bottom of the cage hovered just above the sea. Dribble and Dash clung on to the bars as waves lapped at their feet. They looked at each other and gulped.

"Make yourselves comfortable," said Slugbeard as the trapdoor slammed shut above the brothers. "You could be in there for a very long time..."

CHAPTER EIGHT

"Now what?" said Dribble as they dangled in the cage. "I feel like bait on the end of a fishing line."

"We'll think of something," said Dash hopefully.

"Hello there," said a cheery barnacle that was growing above them on the underside of the hideout. "It's been a while since anyone's been in there. Staying long?"

"We're not on holiday!" Dribble replied angrily. "We're prisoners of these terrible pirates. Do you think they'll set us free?"

"I wouldn't hold your breath waiting for that," said the barnacle. "They're a grumpy lot, those pirates. But I would hold your breath when the weather gets a bit rough, as that cage is underwater most of the time!"

"We have to get out of here, Dribble!" said Dash firmly. "And fast. We need to make a plan."

"I can help," came a voice from beneath them.

Dribble and Dash looked down in surprise and saw Prudence the prawn poking her head out of the water.

"Prudence! What are you doing here?" asked Dash. At the sight of a familiar face, his bottom flashed on and off like some dodgy half-price Christmas tree lights.

"I was on my way home after you freed me from the rock pool," Prudence explained. "Then I saw the pirate ship sailing towards the beach! I thought I'd better warn you, but the pirates got to the beach first. I watched you being taken prisoner, but I didn't know what to do! So I followed the ship to see what happened... If I can help in any way, I will – and so will all my prawn friends. In fact, we're working on something that might help you right now..."

"Thank you," said Dash. "We just need a way to get out of this cell. Because I think I might have come up with an idea that will get us off this island and all the way back to **Bogbrush-on-Sea**..."

But Dash's idea would have to wait. At that moment, they heard the trapdoor above them opening. Prudence ducked out of sight. It was Captain Slugbeard.

"I've made my decision," said the pirate. "After all, you saved us from Big Steve. So, instead of punishing you, I've decided you will stay on **Crabsick Island** and do all our cleaning, cooking and laundry ... for ever."

"Lucky old you!" said the barnacle. "I'll miss your company. Although I wouldn't fancy doing pirate laundry myself. Think of all the underpants that need washing and all the eyepatches you'll have to iron. You'll be working day and night, year in, year out."

Dribble and Dash didn't like the sound of that, but they didn't have any choice in the matter.

"At least it gets us out of this cage," whispered Dash as Slugbeard ordered the burly beetle pirate to drag them out of the cell. "We've a much better chance to escape now."

"I heard that!" roared Slugbeard. "There'll be no escaping, you treacherous toerags! You'll be far too tired to escape after what I've got planned for you."

He led them to the kitchen and pointed at the pots and pans stacked on the stove.

"It's midday and the crew are hungry," he said. "You can start by making us some lunch. And I don't mean soppy little sandwiches with cucumber inside and the crusts cut off, sat on lovely, pretty doilies – although if you find some doilies, I don't mind you using them as they do make everything look classy. I mean proper pirate food like pie, cake and crisps, just like our last cook used to make."

"What happened to the last cook?" asked Dribble.

"He was taken by Big Steve," said Slugbeard sadly. "Poor Botulism Bill! All that was left of him was a half-eaten sausage roll."

"If we're going to be here for ever, can I at least have my **Bubbler** back?" asked Dribble.

"No chance, you dim-witted dolt!" Slugbeard jangled a ring of keys in his sword belt. "I'm locking your contraption in the storeroom so I can look at it properly later. It must be valuable if you're so desperate to get it back. Now get to work – there's a load of hungry pirates that need feeding!"

Dribble and Dash set to the task of making the pirates their lunch. Luckily, Dash knew how to cook, and Dribble knew how to eat, so between them they were able to come up with a meal. But, with so many pirates, it meant a lot of cooking. It was exhausting! Dash would have given anything to see Gus and his fancy air fryer at that moment.

"I hope we can get out of here soon. I don't think I can look at another fish cake," said Dribble as they took the twenty-fifth batch out of the oven. "When can we put our genius escape plan into action?"

"*My* genius escape plan," said Dash as he added an extra dollop of grease to the gravy. "But it does involve you, Dribble."

"I should think so! A genius plan requires a genius, after all."

"Do you remember how we used the **Bubbler** to get us out of that traffic jam?"

Dribble looked confused. "You want to fill this whole place with bubbles so the entire island floats away?" he said.

"No!" said Dash. "But what about a bubble that could carry us away – just the two of us? We could float across the sea and back to land."

"But we don't have any jelly." Dribble frowned.

"We do have that, though," said Dash, pointing to the sink that was overflowing with dirty dishes. There was a big bottle of Lemony Sparkle washing-up liquid next to the taps.

"That's genius-level inspiration! It's a good job I'm here to inspire you. However, I do see one tiny problem. We don't have the **Bubbler**! We'd need to get the key to the storeroom from Slugbeard's belt."

If Dash had sleeves, he would have rolled them up. There was a determined glint in his eye.

"I know," he said grimly. "And that's just what we're going to do."

It was time to serve lunch. Dribble and Dash piled the food on to a wobbly trolley and wheeled it into the dining room, where the pirates were waiting, seated round a long table. They laid the plates of pies and fishcakes in front of the pirates, who tucked in eagerly.

"This is excellent grub!" said one pirate, his mouth full of grease.

"And there'll be plenty more," said Slugbeard, laughing, "as these two lily-livered lard scraps will be staying here permanently!"

"Not if we can help it," muttered Dribble, who was pushing the trolley behind Dash. At that moment, just as they planned, one of its wheels fell off with a clunk. The plates of food toppled from the trolley to the floor with a crash, sending pastry and breadcrumbs flying over the pirates like crusty confetti.

"Oh dear!" said Dribble.

"Watch what you're doing, you puny pie prodder!" roared Slugbeard as Dash swooped in to pick up the plates from around the pirate's chair.

"Sorry, Captain!" said Dash, hiding a gleeful smile.

Luckily, there was still plenty of food to go around. After they'd finished serving, Dribble

and Dash dragged the broken trolley back to the kitchen.

"Did you get it?" asked Dribble.

Dash produced a rusty metal key. "The captain was too busy complaining to notice me unhooking the storeroom key from his belt!" he said with a grin. "It was a genius idea of yours to loosen the wheel on the trolley, Dribble."

"Of course it was!" said Dribble. "You were having far too many good ideas. It was my turn. And no one suspected a thing! Now let's go and get the **Bubbler**."

They peeked out of the kitchen door. The pirates

were engrossed in their meal. They'd be occupied for a while. As silently as possible, the brothers slid past them and out of a door at the side of the dining room.

"The storeroom must be somewhere at the back of the hideout," whispered Dash.

Stealthily, they crept through several untidy rooms. One was a bedroom with tatty hammocks for the pirates to sleep in. Another was a filthy bathroom with mould growing in the shower. No wonder they wanted someone to clean up after them!

"The sooner we get out of here, the better!" grumbled Dribble. "I'm not sharing a toilet with these mucky miscreants!"

Eventually, they found a door with a padlock.

"This must be it!" said Dash. He tried the key and, to their delight, the padlock sprang open.

Quietly, the brothers entered the room.

It was full of food supplies, boxes of junk, and rope and spare parts for the **Norovirus**. And there, sitting on a shelf, was the **Bubbler**.

"We found it!" cried Dribble, getting misty-eyed. "Poor **Bubbler**! I was beginning to think I'd never see you again."

"There's no time for a heartfelt reunion," said Dash urgently. "We need to get back to the kitchen!"

Just then, they heard a roar from the dining room. It was Slugbeard.

"More grub!" came the shout. "Where have those two pathetic pot stirrers got to?"

"They're not in the kitchen!" said one of the pirates.

"They must be trying to escape!" said another.

There was the sound of scurrying footsteps. The pirates were looking for them!

"Uh-oh!" said Dash. "Quick – let's go NOW!"

Dribble grabbed the **Bubbler**, and the pair left the storeroom as fast as they could. They were just making their way down the corridor to the kitchen when they were met by a bunch of angry-looking pirates – some with gravy dribbling down their chins.

"There you are! You devious doily danglers are in trouble," growled Slugbeard. "Get them, shipmates!"

The pirates gave out a yell and began the chase.

The brothers didn't wait around. They hurried back down the corridor and through a doorway that led outside. Dribble slammed the door shut behind them and Dash pushed a barrel in front of it to buy them some time.

"Now what?" gasped Dribble. "There's nothing but sea!"

The secret hideout was made up of several buildings. There was a small windmill and a couple of wooden lookout towers, and even a mast for when the pirates needed to sail **Crabsick Island** to a new location.

"Let's hide in one of the towers," said Dash. "And maybe we can attract the attention of a passing ship."

"It's worth a try!" said Dribble.

Dash flew to the top of the nearest tower and Dribble followed, pulling himself up its ramp.

Meanwhile, the pirates broke through the door and tumbled out on to the raft.

"They're in the crow's nest!" yelled Slugbeard. "After them! There's nowhere for those feisty fugitives to go from there, except down!"

The pirates followed the brothers, some

cautiously climbing the ladder with their cutlasses gripped between their teeth, while others flew in circles round the tower.

Dash glanced about desperately for something to defend themselves with. He grabbed the telescope that was used to keep a lookout – he might be able to fend the pirates off with it. Then he noticed some movement a little way out to sea. He put the telescope to his eye. Somebody was waving at them, trying to attract their attention.

"It's Prudence!" Dash cried. "And she's not alone."

The little prawn was surrounded by many others of her kind. They were dragging something in their claws.

"There's a huge net," said Dash. "I think it goes all the way round the raft. The prawns are carrying it away."

"This is no time for fishing!" snapped Dribble as Dash gave him the telescope. The pirates were getting closer and closer! Then the snail spotted something further out to sea. "Unless you're trying to catch a really big fish. That fin looks very familiar."

"Big Steve!" cried Dash. He shouted down to the pirates: "Big Steve is attacking the hideout!"

From the bottom of the tower, Slugbeard laughed. "**Crabsick Island** is surrounded by powerful Steve-proof nets. Even that monster couldn't get through!"

"Oh dear," said Dash. "I think I might have some news for you..."

CRASH!

With the nets now removed by the prawns, the giant fish swam straight into the raft. The tower shook and several pirates fell from the ramp. The rest scampered back down as quickly as they could.

"How is this possible?" yelled Slugbeard furiously as the raft rocked back and forth.

Before anyone could answer, there was an enormous **CHOMP!** as the giant fish

CRASH!

took a bite out of the raft. Wood splinters flew everywhere. There was another **CHOMP!** and a couple of the smaller sheds collapsed. For a moment, another of the sheds wobbled dangerously ... then, with a sound like someone eating a crisp sandwich, it fell, smashing into the raft's mast. Dribble and Dash watched as the mast lurched from side to side.

"This doesn't look good," said Dash. "I think the mast is going to—"

Before he could finish, the bolts holding the mast in place popped like champagne corks and the huge pole toppled towards the lookout tower like a falling tree.

"Hang on tight, Dribble!" cried Dash. "It's going to hit us!"

CRACK!

CHAPTER TEN

The tower crumpled under the mast, sending the pirates scattering in all directions.

"AIIIIIEEEEEE!" Dribble cried as the floor sped towards them. "We're going to be splatted! Wait – hang on a minute. I'm flying!"

Luckily for Dribble, Dash had grabbed hold of the snail's shell and jumped off the tower before it fell. Dribble was too heavy for him to carry far, but he flapped his little wings as hard as he could, slowing their fall. They landed on the raft with a bump, but safe and sound.

"Splat avoided," said Dribble with relief. "Thank you, Dash!"

"No problem, bro," said Dash.

However, there wasn't time to sit around. Big Steve was still on the attack!

CHOMP! He took another bite out of the raft. And another. The secret hideout was in trouble. Half the jetty was now missing.

"What happened to the nets?" Slugbeard growled at his crew.

"They've vanished!" said a pirate. "It's like someone's pinched them!"

"Villains!" said Slugbeard. "Who'd dare to pinch from a pirate? Launch the **Norovirus**! It's time we dealt with this oversized sardine once and for all!"

Seizing their chance, the brothers sped to the doorway of the main building just as Big Steve rose from the depths and took another chunk out of Slugbeard's secret hideout. Bits of wood and plaster fell around the pair, and the raft trembled as the fish circled it, deciding what to chew next.

The pirates hurried aboard the **Norovirus**, waving their cutlasses in fury, while Slugbeard stood on what was left of the jetty, raging at the state of his domain.

"Load the cannon!" he cried. "We'll get this blundering building-biter if it's the last thing we do!"

Meanwhile, Dribble and Dash had reached the kitchen.

"This is exactly the distraction we needed," said Dash with a grin. "Thanks to Prudence and her friends. Now it's time to put our genius plan into action."

They found a large pot, filled it with washing-up liquid, then stepped into it. Dribble took the **Bubbler** and placed the nozzle into the soap.

"Prepare yourself, Dash," Dribble warned. "This is not going to smell good."

Next, he slowly pressed the button, releasing a steady flow of gas. A shimmering bubble began to form, growing and growing until it completely surrounded them. Thanks to the midge fart gas, the bubble separated from the liquid and began to float, taking the brothers with it!

"Quickly!" said Dash urgently. "We can steer it like a treadmill. Just keep moving in the direction of **Bogbrush-on-Sea**!"

"I don't like flying," Dribble whimpered as the bubble began to glide across the kitchen.

"Don't worry!" said Dash. "We'll soon be back on land, and this will all be over."

"I hope so," said Dribble as Dash steered the bubble out of the open door. "But what if we always have bad luck because of Slugbeard's curse? The Dung Heap Gang may have stolen the treasure, but we found it!"

The bubble wobbled its way out of the building and floated along the jetty into the air. The breeze took it, and the brothers sailed into the sky.

Below them, the **Norovirus** was in brave pursuit of Big Steve. Dribble and Dash watched as a cloud of smoke burst from the side of the ship, followed by a loud booming sound. A cannon had fired! But instead of a cannonball, a giant net launched into the air. It spread out as it flew, landing over a surprised Big Steve. He was caught!

As the pirates busily secured the net round the fish, who thrashed about in a rage, Slugbeard spotted the bubble flying overhead.

"Those food-flinging nincompoops are getting away!" he yelled. "Forget the fish, we can come back for him later. I want those two caught. We haven't even finished lunch yet and we've already lost another set of kitchen staff!"

Dribble and Dash attempted to steer the bubble away from the island, but even though the wind was behind them it was hard work.

"I'm not sure how long I can carry on!" Dash said. "I'll be worn out by the time we get back to **Bogbrush-on-Sea**! That wasn't part of my genius idea."

"That's why you should leave the genius ideas to me!" said Dribble. "If we don't steer, we'll float up into the sky and won't stop until we hit the moon. There's no cabbage there for me to eat and I'll be hungry!"

The snail hopped about nervously. The bubble shook dangerously...

"Don't do that, Dribble," warned Dash. "Or the bubble will—"

The soapy bubble couldn't take the strain and exploded in a burst of lemony freshness. The two bugs plummeted into the sea below...

And landed with an enormous splash.

Dash coughed and spluttered. He tried to fly, but his wings were soaked.

"Help!" cried Dribble, bobbing about in the water using his shell as a lifeboat. "I don't want to be fish food!"

They were in the middle of the sea, far from anywhere, and there was no sign of any rescue. What would become of them?

CHAPTER ELEVEN

"Grab that piece of wood!" Dash said, pointing to a broken plank floating towards them. "Wait – that looks familiar."

"It's the 'secret hideout' sign from **Crabsick Island**," said Dribble, clambering on to it. "How did that get here?"

At that moment, Prudence appeared in the water beside them, along with loads of other prawns.

"Surprise!" Prudence said with a grin. "I thought you two land bugs might need help getting away. You're not exactly made for life at sea! So we took a bit of the wreckage from the pirates' home for you to use as a raft."

"Thank you!" said Dash. "You've probably saved our lives!"

"My friends and I can take you all the way back to **Bogbrush-on-Sea**. But we'd better get moving as the pirates are already on their way."

Sure enough, the sails of the **Norovirus** were visible not far behind.

The prawns crowded round the sign and began to push, flapping their tails so that it glided across the water. Dribble and Dash bounced around on top.

"This is actually fun!" Dribble said, laughing. "Sailing is much better than flying!"

Soon the prawn-powered raft was moving at speed and the brothers watched as the seaside town appeared on the horizon in front of them. They were almost there!

"Thank you so much for all your help," Dash said to Prudence as the raft neared the harbour. "It was you who removed the anti-Steve nets from round the pirate's island, wasn't it?"

"Yes!" said Prudence gleefully. "The pirates are no friends of ours. Big Steve was more than happy to cause trouble. Right now, some of my prawn friends are helping him out of that net the pirates used to catch him. He'll be waiting for them when they get back home – or whatever's left of it!"

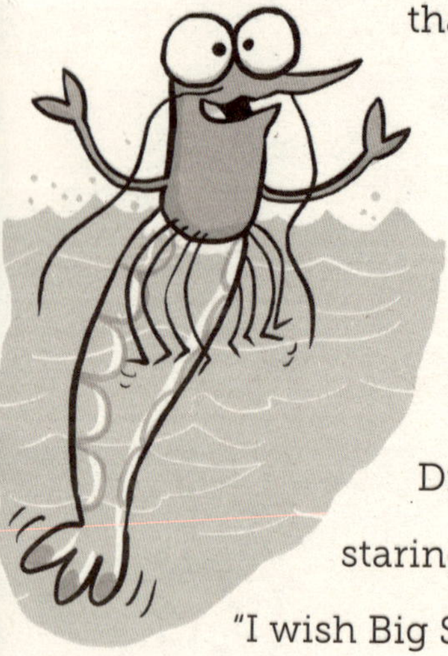

Dash was just about to breathe a sigh of relief when Dribble gave a yelp. The snail was staring out to sea, terror in his eyes.

"I wish Big Steve was waiting here instead," he said. "Because those snozdigging pirates are right behind us!"

Dash turned to see the wide white sails of the **Norovirus** looming over them and the skull-and-crossbones flag grinning wickedly in the breeze.

"There's no escape from old Slugbeard, you wriggling weasels!" roared the pirate captain. "Soon you'll be back in that kitchen, and I'll see to it that you'll have so much washing-up to do your fingers will look like wrinkled prunes FOR EVER!"

"No!" cried Dash. "We're never going back. Look, Dribble! We're almost at the beach!"

The prawns gave the life raft one last almighty push, and it sailed towards the sand. Dribble and Dash clung on tightly.

"Now's our chance, shipmates!" yelled Slugbeard to his crew. "Get them!"

The raft crashed on to the sand and Dash was thrown sideways.

"Help!" Dribble said. "How do you stop this thing?"

Suddenly the broken sign hit a rock, flipping over and sending Dribble somersaulting into the air. The **Bubbler** somersaulted with him, before falling to the ground with a clatter. Dribble followed. He fell heavily, landing right on the Maximum Power setting and crushing the gadget's nozzle.

"Oh no!" said Dribble as the **Bubbler** began to rattle and shake. "The fart gas is trapped. The pressure is building... I think the **Bubbler** is going to explode!"

"I suppose it had to happen at some point," said Dash wearily.

At that moment, the **Bubbler** ruptured – and a rush of fart gas erupted from its insides.

KWWAAAAAAAAKKK!!

It was the loudest fart **Bogbrush-on-Sea** had ever heard. Even louder than the last one.

It blew across the beach, sweeping clouds of sand in all directions, and engulfed the **Norovirus**, filling its sails full of fetid wind. The pirates yelled and held on tight to the masts as their ship was carried away, blown far out to sea by the foul-smelling hurricane. In a matter of seconds, they were nothing more than a speck on the horizon.

Stunned, Dribble and Dash picked themselves up off the ground.

"We've ... escaped!" said Dash. "We actually escaped! We can go home now, Dribble. At last!"

But his brother just stared at the remains of the **Bubbler**.

"It's destroyed," Dribble said forlornly. "Cool Nat can't use it now. This trip was all for nothing."

"Never mind," said Dash. "The most important thing is that we're safe."

The brothers said their goodbyes to Prudence and the other prawns, who were playing in the surf.

"This has been quite an adventure," said Dash. "Thank you again for rescuing us, Prudence."

"You rescued me first, don't forget!" the prawn replied. "This has been the most fun me and my prawn besties have had in ages. Those silly pirates needed putting in their place. We don't mind sharing the sea, but not with those bullies. They'll be far too busy avoiding Big Steve to come back to shore any time soon."

"I hope we see each other again next time we're by the sea," said Dash. "I'd like to see how the sea bugs live."

The prawns waved their claws before sinking back into the waves.

There were shouts from further down the beach. It was Taneesha, Gus, Tilda and Reg, along with Sergeant Buzabiz.

"We saw what happened from the pier!" said Tilda.

"Were those actual pirates? Are you two all right?" said Taneesha.

"That was Slugbeard!" cried Dribble. He sighed heavily. "We're fine, but the **Bubbler** is in tiny little pieces."

"We were saved by Dribble's invention exploding," explained Dash. No one looked surprised. "We'll tell you the story later."

"There's a police boat going off to chase down those no-good saltwater criminals," said Sergeant Buzabiz. "Funnily enough, the police conference was all about tackling pirate-related crime. Slugbeard will soon be behind bars."

They heard the toot of the horn from the slugs' bus from up on the promenade. Flattened Dominic was at the wheel.

"I suppose we should head back to **Bugtown**," said Gus, scratching his smooth bum.

"What about the seaweed?" asked Tilda. "Nat still needs to practise for his competition."

"And I still want my favourite smoothie!" added Taneesha.

"We did collect it earlier," Dash said. "But then it was scattered all over the beach by the blast from the **Bubbler**."

"There are more of us here now," said Taneesha. "We'll soon finish the job."

The bugs helped to gather up the seaweed. Flattened Dominic grumbled about it being loaded into the bus, but there was still be plenty of room for everyone.

Suddenly they heard police sirens coming from further along the promenade.

A moment later, two police cars appeared, driving very fast. But they weren't chasing criminals – one car was chasing the other!

"What the Neddikins is going on?" said Sergeant Buzabiz.

The first police car zoomed towards them, heading straight for the last pile of seaweed waiting to be loaded.

"Everybody out of the way!" shouted Sergeant Buzabiz.

The startled bugs jumped to safety, but the car was going too fast to stop in time and ploughed through the wet, slippery leaves. It skidded and then spun to a halt, right by the bus. The second police car screeched to a stop beside it. Police bugs leapt out and surrounded the seaweed-covered vehicle.

"What's going on?" said Taneesha, waving her arms like a distressed crayon.

"Come out with your hands up!" shouted a police bug. "You're under arrest for stealing police property and generally being very naughty! Although that skid was really cool."

The driver's door slowly opened ... and out stepped Netty and Lou, looking glum. Mr Truffle was in the back seat, quietly glowering.

"If it isn't the Dung Heap Gang," said Sergeant Buzabiz with a chuckle. "And trying to steal a police car too. What a cheeky bunch of criminals!"

"It was Mr Truffle's idea," grumbled Netty. "We needed some transport to carry all the pirate treasure we pinched... Oops!"

Lou groaned. "So much for our quiet, low-profile holiday," she said.

"You can look forward to a holiday in **Bugtown** Jail," said the police bee, getting out his handcuffs. "A very long holiday."

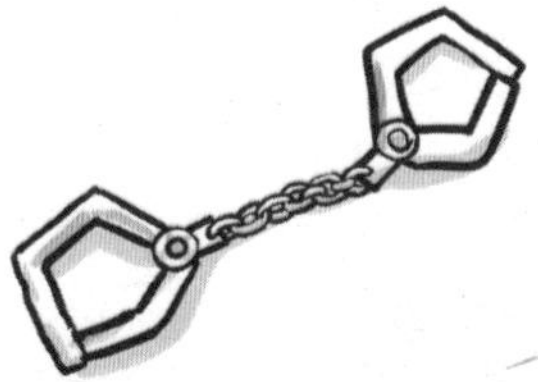

"It turns out the curse of Slugbeard was real, after all," Dash said to Dribble as the gang were led away.

"Oh, don't be silly," said Dribble with a smirk. "There's no such thing as curses..."

*

All the bugs were pleased to be heading back home to **Bugtown.** They were in such a good mood that no one objected to Taneesha's suggestion of a singalong – at least not for the first few minutes. Thankfully, there were no snoozing pigeons on the road or any other disruptions, because Sergeant Buzabiz gave them a police escort the whole way as a thank you for stopping the Dung Heap Gang. The bus made it back to Grottibottigan's just in time for a late-afternoon smoothie.

"I feel for you, dudes," said Cool Nat when he heard about Dribble and Dash's adventures. "Pirates are seriously unchill, in my experience."

He was delighted with the seaweed delivery and gave everyone free drinks for the rest of the month, as promised. And a week later, when he'd won at the **Juice Barista Championships** with his Surf and Turf smoothie, he gave everyone free drinks for the next month too.

In spite of the prospect of lots of free cabbage juice, Dribble was still downhearted about his broken **Bubbler**.

"What can I do to cheer him up?" Dash asked the others as they celebrated with Cool Nat at Grottibottigan's.

Unexpectedly, it was Reg who came up with the answer. As they were leaving the juice bar, he quietly drew Dribble to one side.

"Dominic and I might have a business proposition for you," he said. "Even if Cool Nat doesn't use your **Bubbler**, we will."

"You?" said Dribble suspiciously. "I hope you're not going to use it for anything naughty."

"Absolutely not, matey," said Reg with a wink. "If you can make a couple more of your gadgets for us, with a few special adjustments, all will be revealed..."

A few days later, Dribble had managed to make three more **Bubblers**. He and Dash took the gadgets to the **Bugtown** park, where they'd agreed to meet Reg, Flattened Dominic and the others. It was all very mysterious. The slugs still hadn't told Dribble what they wanted his invention for.

"I hope they're not opening a juice bar," said Dash. "Cool Nat won't like the competition."

"I don't think that's what they're up to," said Dribble. "They made me change the **Bubbler**'s design. It's too big to fit in a smoothie glass now."

When they arrived at the park, they saw their friends standing around a large basket, with a huge bag lying next to it.

"What's going on?" asked Dribble. "What is this thing?"

"It's a balloon!" said Reg. "It's our new business venture: **Slugtours Fart-Powered Adventures**!"

"We're still brainstorming the name," said Dominic. "We got the idea from our trip to **Bogbrush-on-Sea**. Looking at the world from above as we floated along in the bus gave us a whole new perspective. So we're going to offer balloon trips. And we need your invention to do it."

"For a share of the profits, of course, matey," said Reg, after a nudge from Tilda. "And you two get to have the first ride."

Dribble was impressed. "That is a genius idea!" he said. And he meant it.

Using the newly redesigned **Bubbler**, the slugs filled the bag with gas. Once it was properly inflated, they attached it to the basket.

"Jump aboard!" said Reg. "And let's leave these landlubbers behind."

Dribble and Dash climbed into the basket, followed by the slugs. The others watched as the balloon rose into the air. Dribble was nervous about flying, but after a gentle take-off he soon calmed down. The balloon climbed higher and higher, and it wasn't long before the brothers could see the whole of **Bugtown** stretched out below.

"Reg is right," said Dash. "Being up here does put a different perspective on the world."

"This is what **Bugtown** must look like to humans," said Dribble.

"I wonder what they think about us bugs," said Dash. "And I wonder if they know just how many stories are taking place so far beneath them."

"I'm sure they do," said Dribble with a grin. "Even if they aren't geniuses like us."

FASCINATING BUG FACTS

WITH PROFESSOR CRISPIN T. EARTHWORM

BUGS DO FART

It's difficult to measure insect farts because they are so tiny, but it is known that many insects do produce back-door breezes! The larvae of the beaded lacewing feed on termites, and it's thought the larvae might stun the termites with their powerful bottom burps!

PRAWNS AREN'T SEA BUGS

But they do have some distant bug relatives. Prawns are a type of creature called a crustacean and are related to crabs and lobsters, but also to woodlice, which live on land.

BUT THERE ARE SEA BUGS

Lots of insects live in ponds and rivers, but only one type of insect lives in the sea. It's called a sea skater, or ocean strider, and it runs across the surface of the sea to catch its prey.

SOME BUGS USE BUBBLES

Certain types of water beetle carry bubbles of air with them when they are diving to allow them to breathe while they are looking for food.

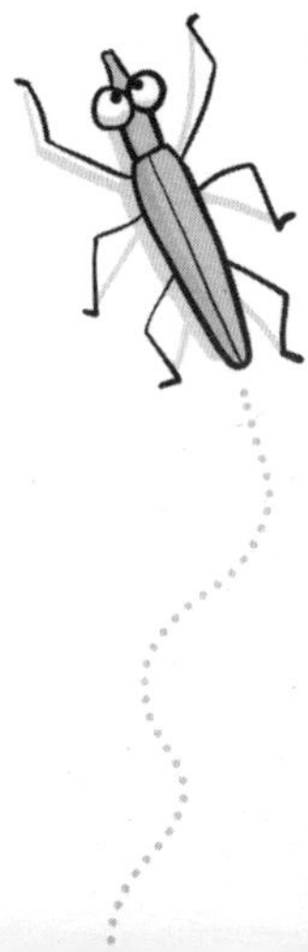

PIRATE NAME

1.

Select the word next to the first letter of your first name:

A – WINDY
B – CAPTAIN
C – SALTY
D – BIG
E – GOLDTOOTH
F – OLD
G – RANDOM
H – FISHY
I – TINY
J – SMELLY
K – KNUCKLES
L – CRABCAKE
M – FLIPPERS
N – WETNOSE
O – SLIMYTOES
P – DANCING
Q – DAINTY
R – WIBBLY
S – FANCY
T – INKY
U – SQUIDFACE
V – CUT-THROAT
W – TOOTHLESS
X – ADMIRAL
Y – JAUNTY
Z – ITCHY

2.

Next, select the word next to your birth month:

JAN – MCGROBBLE
FEB – O'PORRIDGE
MAR – BOFFCLAPPER
APR – GIZZARDSNAPPER
MAY – FIDDLEBOTTOM
JUN – GRANNYBEARD
JUL – PARROTSQUAWK
AUG – JAMMYFINGER
SEP – O'BOGEY
OCT – BOGBOTHERER
NOV – QUACKSPLATTER
DEC – CORKPOPPER

GENERATOR

Follow these instructions to create your own pirate name!

3.

Finally, select the word next to the last letter of your last name.
Put the three together to make your pirate name!

A – THE TERRIFYING
B – THE BOLD
C – THE FORGETFUL
D – THE QUITE PLEASANT
E – THE LEGENDARY
F – THE QUICK
G – THE TYRANT
H – THE LOUD
I – THE DAFT
J – THE TALKATIVE
K – THE VERY NAUGHTY
L – THE MERMAID'S FRIEND
M – THE SHARK WHISPERER
N – THE GOLD SNIFFER
O – THE JEWELLED
P – THE OCEAN WALKER
Q – THE GHOST
R – THE BONE CHOMPER
S – THE OCTOPUS WRESTLER
T – THE BLUE PHANTOM
U – THE SEAWEED CHEWER
V– THE LOBSTER WRANGLER
W – THE VINEGARY
X – THE BARRACUDA
Y – THE DROOLER
Z – THE GREEN TERROR

MAKE YOUR OWN BUG HOTEL

Dribble and Dash and their friends stayed at the fancy **Bedbug Hotel** in **Bogbrush-on-Sea**.

Here are some instructions on how to make a hotel for real bugs! It's less fancy, but bugs will love it. A bug hotel gives shelter to insects in winter and is a safe place for them to lay their eggs.

1 Cut the ends off a plastic bottle to make a tube. This is tricky, so get a grown-up to do it. If the bottle is large, you might be able to make two hotels from it.

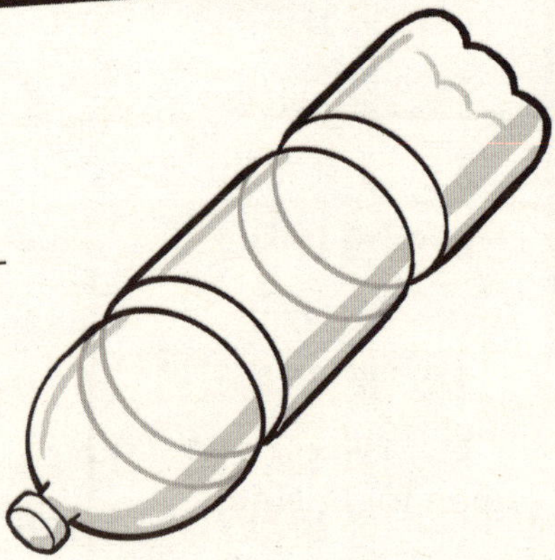

2 Loop a piece of string round the tube to make a handle, so the hotel can be hung on a tree or fence post.

3 Pack the tube tightly with sticks, tree bark, rolled-up cardboard, pine cones, moss, pieces of bamboo, straw and dry leaves. Make sure they're packed tight enough, so they won't fall out.

4 Hang the hotel in a warm, sunny spot. Your hotel is open for business!

STORY STARTERS

Here are some ideas to start you off writing your own stories. You can write about Dribble and Dash and their friends, or try making up your own characters instead!

1 Write a story about the **Bugtown** Juice Barista Championships. You could write about Cool Nat or Janice the moth, or a character of your own. Think up a recipe for a smoothie that could be entered into the competition. What could go wrong? Perhaps the blender explodes, or the wrong ingredient is added. Disaster! Or maybe another barista tries to cheat! What happens next? Who would win the competition and what's the prize?

2 Reg Scribble and Flattened Dominic have a new business offering balloon tours. Describe one of their tours. Where does it go? Make up a destination and write about what it's like. It could be a seaside town or a spooky forest or a mountain castle. What do the passengers see? Who do they meet? Do they get back home safely?

3 Write about one of the voyages of the **Norovirus** and its pirate crew. They could be following a map to buried treasure on a desert island. What adventures do they have? They could meet a sea monster like Big Steve along the way, or treacherous mer-slugs, or rival pirates hunting the same treasure. Describe what the island is like – perhaps there's a jungle or a volcano! Do they find the treasure?

4 Prudence the prawn lives in **Shrimpville**, an underwater town full of sea creatures. Write about a day in her life. Describe her family and friends – what kind of creatures are they? What is **Shrimpville** like? It could be a coral reef or maybe an old sunken ship covered in barnacles. What happens when there's a storm? Or when a shark comes to visit? Think of all the ways that living underwater might affect your life.

ARE THOSE MY PANTS?

David O'Connell

is a crazy old man who writes and draws books. He likes comics, TV shows about space, and sitting in his garden talking to all the bugs that live there. Sometimes they talk back, or so he thinks.

ACKNOWLEDGEMENTS

I'd like to acknowledge all the teachers, librarians and booksellers who work so hard every day to get books into young readers' hands – thank you so much! Thanks also to all the readers who have told me how much they enjoy Dribble and Dash's adventures – I really appreciate it. A big thank you to my agent, Jodie Hodges, and all my lovely supportive friends and family.

BEASTIE BROS

is a

Scholastic Books

Production

David O'Connell

Writer and illustrator

David says: So many people helped to put this book together! I'd like to thank Julia Sanderson, Sarah Baldwin, Wendy Shakespeare, Olivia Towers, Hannah Love, Holly Clarke, Rosie Watts, Alice Pagin and all the brilliant folk at Scholastic.

DON'T MISS DRIBBLE AND DASH'S FIRST ADVENTURE

David O'Connell
HE'S AS DAFT AS A GNAT!
BEASTIE BROS
THE CABBAGE JUICE CRIME

AND CHECK OUT THEIR HEROIC JOURNEY INTO HIDDEN KINGDOMS...

David O'Connell
BEASTIE BROS
DUNGEONS AND DRAGONFLIES